The Old Tree Stories

Hungry Mr. Fox

Published by
Delacorte Press
The Bantam Doubleday Dell Publishing Group, Inc.
666 Fifth Avenue
New York, New York 10103

First published in Great Britain by Belitha Press Ltd.,
31 Newington Green, London N16 9PU.

Conceived, designed and produced by Belitha Press Ltd.

Text and illustrations copyright © Peter Firmin 1989

Library of Congress Cataloging-in-Publication Data

Firmin, Peter.
  Hungry Mr. Fox/Peter Firmin.
    p. cm. – (The old tree stories)
  Summary: Hungry Mr. Fox captures and releases a succession of
animals, always hoping to catch something bigger and juicier, until
he makes a big mistake.
  ISBN 0-440-50034-6
  [1. Foxes – Fiction.   2. Animals – Fiction.]   I. Series.
PZ7.F49873Hu   1989
[E] – dc19   88-3871
                                                        CIP
                                                        AC

Manufactured in Hong Kong
June 1989
10 9 8 7 6 5 4 3 2 1

PETER FIRMIN

The Old Tree Stories

Hungry Mr. Fox

Delacorte Press

Mr. Fox was hiding at the bottom
of the Old Tree.
He said, "I'd like something tasty
for dinner."

There was a fence near the tree.
There was a gap in the fence.
Through the gap came
a plump little mouse.

Mr. Fox jumped out.
He caught the mouse and said,
"I'll gobble you up for
my dinner, nibble, nibble!"

The mouse said,
"Oh, don't spoil your dinner
with a mouthful like me.
There's a much better
meal coming soon."
So he let the mouse go.

Mr. Fox waited at the bottom
of the Old Tree.
He said, "I shall have something
tasty for my dinner."

Through the gap in the fence came a very fat rat.

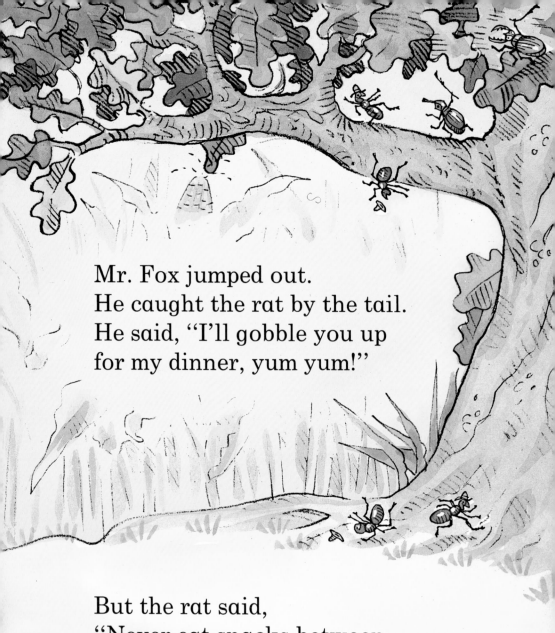

Mr. Fox jumped out.
He caught the rat by the tail.
He said, "I'll gobble you up
for my dinner, yum yum!"

But the rat said,
"Never eat snacks between
meals. Besides, there's someone
much fatter back there."

So Mr. Fox let the rat go.

Mr. Fox waited at the bottom of the Old Tree. He said, "I *must* have something tasty for my dinner."

Through the gap in the fence,
with a leap and a jump, came a hare,
and Mr. Fox said, "Now, here's
something tasty for dinner!"

Mr. Fox grabbed her
and held her and said,
"I'll gobble you up for
my dinner, SNAP, SNAP!"

The hare said, "Don't you think
I'd unsettle your tum? There's
something much bigger back there."
So he let the hare go.

Mr. Fox waited and what did he see?
A big brown whiskery nose.

He jumped out and grabbed it,
and bit it and said,
"You're not a mouse, rat or hare
but whatever you are,
I'll gobble you up
for my dinner, CRUNCH, CRUNCH!"

A big angry bear jumped
out through the gap.
He said, "You greedy old fox.
You'd better not gobble
the mouse or the rat
or the hare . . .
and especially not ME!"

He tossed
Mr. Fox
high up into
the tree . . .

and the mouse and the hare and
the rat and the bear went
into the field for their dinner,
MUNCH, MUNCH.